THE SCARS WE SHARE

YASHVARDHAN SINGH

Thank You Franz Kafka.

Thank You Fyodor Dostoevsky.

Thank You Friedrich Nietzsche.

Contents

Foreword

From the Depths I Wrote: How I Survived the Darkest Hours Through Literature

There is a certain kind of darkness that does not come with thunder or lightning. It arrives softly, insidiously, like a cold mist that creeps through cracks, filling every corner until it suffocates light itself. This darkness is the weight you feel pressing on your chest in the dead of night, the silence so deep it roars inside your head, the loneliness so absolute it seems to swallow your very soul.

I know this darkness intimately — not as a visitor, but as a captor. It held me in its cold embrace when life itself became a hollow echo. I was not plunged into it suddenly, like a victim of catastrophe or trauma. No, my descent was slow, deliberate, and without mercy — like being buried alive, inch by inch, until the world I knew was nothing but a faint memory.

To be trapped in that darkness is to lose yourself. The "I" that once existed becomes a distant, flickering candle, barely visible through the oppressive night. You question everything: your purpose, your worth, your very existence. The mind, usually a refuge of logic and hope, becomes a labyrinth of shadows where sinister thoughts lurk, whispering poison in your ear.

In those hours, when your skin feels thinner than paper and every breath is a struggle against unseen chains, the world outside carries on — vibrant, warm, and indifferent. People smile, laugh, and live as if the abyss does not exist. But inside, you are drowning in silence. The abyss is a living thing, with teeth and claws. It knows your fears, your regrets, your weaknesses. It feasts on your pain and leaves behind only numbness.

I was there, deep inside that darkness, where time dilated and minutes stretched into eternal torture. The weight of despair was so suffocating that I felt my ribs might crack, my lungs might collapse. There were moments when I thought death might be the only escape, the final release from this nightmare.

But I did not die.

Somewhere, in the void where my soul had almost given up, I found a trembling hand extended toward me — literature.

The books were unassuming at first. Old, dog-eared volumes picked up in abandoned libraries or dusty corners of secondhand stores. I was not looking for salvation; I was looking for distraction, a temporary escape from the noise in my head.

But the words, strange and stubborn, began to penetrate the darkness. They were not simple comforts. They were not naive platitudes about hope or happiness. They were shadows and flames, truths wrapped in riddles, stories told in voices that understood pain.

There was horror in those pages — not the kind that makes your skin crawl or your heart race with adrenaline. It was the horror of human fragility, the terror of being utterly alone inside your own mind, the quiet madness that creeps into the soul when you cannot escape yourself.

One night, I read a passage from Lovecraft — not for his monsters or mythos, but for the way he described the cosmic indifference to human suffering. The universe was vast and uncaring, and that realization was a kind of darkness itself. But it was honest. It stripped away the false hope that I had been clinging to and replaced it with a raw truth: pain is part of existence. The abyss is real.

It terrified me, but it also freed me.

Because if pain and darkness are real, then so too is the possibility of survival.

I began to read voraciously, pulling myself into worlds that reflected the shadows I knew. Poe's macabre tales spoke of madness and despair; the confessions of Dostoevsky wrestled with guilt and redemption; the raw poems of Sylvia Plath bled honesty and fractured beauty.

These voices, so haunted and fractured, became my companions. They whispered that I was not unique in my suffering, that others had looked into the abyss and lived to tell the tale. But more importantly, they showed me that the abyss could be a place of transformation — a place where the broken could be remade.

I began to write — at first barely more than scrawls on scraps of paper, later paragraphs and pages filled with the dark musings of a fractured mind. Writing was terrifying; it forced me to face the monsters lurking inside. But it was also a kind of exorcism.

I wrote of the shadows that followed me, of the voices in my head that twisted my thoughts like serpents. I wrote of loneliness that was not just absence, but a living entity — cold and calculating, waiting for me to falter. I wrote of moments when despair felt like a physical presence, sitting on my chest, whispering that I was beyond help.

But I also wrote of moments of fragile light — a memory, a line of poetry, the flicker of a thought that maybe I could endure.

In the darkest nights, literature was the only light I could hold onto. It was not bright or blazing — it was a candle in the storm, trembling but persistent.

Sometimes the words offered no comfort. Sometimes they were mirrors reflecting my deepest fears back at me.

But in facing those fears, I began to reclaim my story.

The abyss remained, always lurking at the edges of my vision, but it no longer controlled me.

The transformation was not miraculous. It was brutal and slow. It was crawling out of a grave one painful inch at a time. It was the kind of survival that leaves scars but also carves strength.

I realized that life itself is a story — and I had the power to tell mine.

Literature gave me a vocabulary for the darkness. It gave me permission to feel everything without shame. It gave me the courage to share my story, not as a tale of defeat but of resilience.

The horror of despair is not just in the suffering, but in the silence — the feeling that no one hears your screams, that you are invisible even to yourself.

Literature breaks that silence. It listens, it witnesses, it remembers.

It saved me.

Poem: The Whispering Dark

The darkness came without a sound,
A creeping chill beneath the ground,
A shadow stretched across my soul,
A silent scream that swallowed whole.

No monster came with claws or teeth,
Just silence deep as ocean's reef,
A void where light refused to grow,
And time moved slow, too slow to know.

But in that dark, a voice did rise —
Not from earth, nor from the skies,
But from the ink where secrets hide,
A whispered hope, a rising tide.

Through pages torn and words that bleed,
I found the strength to plant a seed,
A fragile flame against the night,
A way to hold on, hold on tight.
So if you dwell where shadows creep,
And feel the dark pull you deep,
Remember: even in the stark,
There lives a light — the whispering dark.

CHAPTER I

The Poet & The Bear

The Scars We Share

-Yashvardhan Singh

Inspired by the story "On the Face of It"

The village of Khadipur was a quaint place nestled between a winding river and a sprawling forest teeming with wild animals. Life here was slow, with the air filled with the scent of damp earth and the murmur of flowing water. But if there was one topic that stirred whispers among the villagers, it was the enigmatic poet, Viraj.

Near the village's tea stall, two men, Prakash and Lallan, sat on wooden benches, sipping their steaming cups of chai. Their conversation, as usual, turned to Viraj.

"Have you seen him today?" Prakash asked, smirking. "Always wandering around with that notebook, muttering to himself. What a sight he is!"

Lallan chuckled. "Oh, you mean the scarecrow? Tall, thin as a stick, dark as midnight, and with that ridiculous hairline—or what's left of it. I swear, the man's forehead is halfway to his neck now."

The two burst into laughter, drawing curious glances from passersby.

"You know," Prakash continued, lowering his voice conspiratorially, "he wasn't always like this. Viraj used to live in the city when he was a boy. But the kids there bullied him mercilessly. Called him all sorts of names, mocked his poems, and made his life miserable. That's why he's hiding out here in the middle of nowhere."

"And now he thinks he's some kind of genius," Lallan scoffed. "Writing about trees and animals like they're his best friends. No wonder he stays alone."

Their laughter faded as a shadow fell over their table. Turning, they saw Viraj himself standing there, clutching his battered notebook. His deep-set eyes lingered on them for a moment before he turned and walked away, his long strides carrying him toward the riverbank. His thin frame seemed to disappear into the mist rising from the water, leaving the men silent and slightly uncomfortable.

Viraj's days were spent wandering through the forest and along the river, observing the world with a quiet intensity. While the villagers mocked his solitude, Viraj found solace in the whispers of the trees and the songs of the birds. Nature, unlike people, did not judge. And in its embrace, Viraj wove his words into verses that spoke of beauty, pain, and the resilience of the human spirit.

Prakash and Lallan were still snickering, but the sound of something heavy splashing in the river caught their attention. The two men looked up just in time to see a bear emerging from the water, its movements slow and labored. It was unlike any bear they had ever seen—its fur was matted and patchy, the deep scars of old wounds marking its sides like a jagged map of suffering. One ear was half torn, and its eyes, dull and bloodshot, carried an eerie, hollow emptiness. The bear's once-majestic appearance had been ravaged by time and battle, leaving behind a creature that seemed more miserable than menacing.

"Good God, look at that thing," Lallan muttered, a shiver crawling down his spine. "It's... it's ugly. What happened to it?"

The bear lumbered forward, stepping onto the shore of the village, its claws digging into the earth with a sad, almost defeated rhythm. Prakash's breath caught in his throat. "Is it... coming this way?"

Before Lallan could respond, panic exploded. "RUN!" he screamed, his voice cracking as he leaped from the bench and bolted, dragging Prakash with him. Villagers who had been lounging nearby scattered in all directions, their cries of fear rising like a chorus of terror. Children wailed, and women shrieked as they ran towards the safety of their homes or toward the nearby hills, seeking shelter from the unknown threat.

Prakash and Lallan, along with the others, dashed toward the edge of the village, their hearts racing as they glanced back to see the bear dragging itself slowly toward them, its gaze unwavering. The sight of the beast, battered and wretched, only added to the fear that gripped the villagers. Its slow movements seemed to foreshadow some inevitable tragedy.

In his small, modest house, Viraj heard the screams—a cacophony of fear that shattered the stillness of the village. His mind flickered with unease, a chill running through him as he grabbed the old, rusted knife he kept by his door. The knife was nothing more than a relic, but in that moment, it was all he had.

He stepped outside, the cold air biting at his skin, his heart thumping in his chest. His gaze swept over the village square, where villagers were scrambling in a frenzy, and then he saw it. The bear, dragging its battered body across the ground, moving toward the village with a strange, sorrowful dignity.

Viraj froze, his eyes locking with the creature's. There was no aggression in the bear's movements, no hunger in its gaze. It wasn't the wild beast the villagers feared, but a broken, abandoned soul, much like him. Viraj felt a deep, unexpected sympathy. He lowered the knife, feeling a strange pull toward the creature, despite the fear it had stirred in the village.

He stepped forward cautiously, his voice barely a whisper. "You're not here to harm anyone, are you?"

The bear gave no answer. It simply stood there, its heavy breaths the only sound in the otherwise silent village. Viraj approached slowly, his gaze softening as he saw the pain etched into every line of the bear's body. It was an image of misery, not malice.

Viraj approached the bear, his feet crunching on the dry earth as he stepped closer. The bear didn't move, its tired eyes watching him intently. There was an air of resignation around it, a sadness that mirrored something deep within Viraj's own soul. He took a breath and crouched a few feet away, lowering his knife.

"Hello," Viraj said gently, his voice low, trying not to startle the creature. "Are you... lost?"

The bear's eyes flickered, and then, to Viraj's surprise, it spoke. The words were gruff, laced with sorrow, as if the bear had carried its pain for years without an outlet.

"Lost?" The bear's voice sounded like gravel scraping against stone. "I've been lost all my life." The bear looked down at its scarred body, the remnants of fur falling in patches, the deep wounds from old encounters with hunters still visible. "The others... they mock me. They call me ugly, call me 'the outcast.' They say I look like a monster."

Viraj's heart tightened. He could feel the rawness in the bear's words. "Why do they call you that?" he asked softly, intrigued by the story hidden beneath the animal's bitterness.

The bear sighed, its broad chest rising and falling heavily. "Because of these," it said, pawing at the deep scars along its side. "The hunter's bullets. The wounds that should have healed... but now, all I see in the reflection of the river is a creature no one can love."

Viraj frowned, feeling a pang of empathy. "That's awful," he murmured. "No one should judge you for that."

The bear looked up at him, its eyes glistening with unspoken emotion. "It's not just the wounds. It's how I look. It's how everyone sees me. I'm an embarrassment. I was born one way, and now... now I'm a shadow of what I could have been. No matter where I go, the others push me away."

Viraj sat silently for a moment, then nodded. "I understand that. More than you think." He looked at the bear with a mixture of sympathy and resolve. "You know, I've had my own share of that. People called me ugly too. Not because of anything I did, but because of how I looked. When I was a child, the city kids would tease me, mock my poems, laugh at me just because I was different."

The bear tilted its head, its expression softening just slightly. "They did that to you? But you're... human."

Viraj chuckled bitterly. "Doesn't matter. I had black gums, teeth too big for my mouth, and my skin was all wrong. It didn't matter what I said or did. The kids saw me and just... laughed."

The bear blinked, considering this. "But you're still here, aren't you?"

"I am," Viraj replied with quiet pride. "I stayed. But it wasn't easy. I spent a lot of time hiding, thinking maybe if I stayed out of sight, no one would laugh at me. And like you, I started to believe that maybe I was broken. That maybe I deserved to be alone."

The bear looked at him with a deep, knowing gaze. "What changed?"

Viraj smiled faintly, gazing out toward the village. "I came here. I left the city, came to the village, and... I found peace in the silence. No one here knows what I used to look like, or who I used to be. And now, the trees, the river, the birds—they don't care about my face. They only care about what I say."

The bear huffed softly. "You're right. Nature doesn't care. But the others... they never stop judging."

Viraj nodded. "People can be cruel, yes. But they don't know you. They don't see the things you've been through. And just because someone calls you ugly doesn't mean you have to believe them."

The bear grunted, its shoulders slumping a little. "Maybe... maybe it's too late for me. I've been beaten down too much."

Viraj stood up and walked slowly around the bear, his voice filled with quiet conviction. "It's never too late. You can still change the way you see yourself. And you can still find your place, no matter what others think."

Just as Viraj finished speaking, a faint snicker echoed from behind him. Turning, he saw Prakash and Lallan standing at a distance, watching him. They were leaning against the old stone wall, their eyes wide in mock disbelief.

"Look at that," Prakash said, a smirk on his face. "The poet's talking to a bear like it's some kind of friend."

Lallan snickered. "Next, he'll start writing poems for it."

They both burst into laughter, not bothering to hide their amusement. "What's he doing, sharing his sad poems with the poor beast?" Lallan mocked, his voice loud enough for Viraj to hear.

Viraj ignored them, turning back to the bear, who was now watching the men, confused. The poet stood tall, as if protecting both himself and the creature from the judgment of others.

"They don't understand," Viraj murmured softly, as much to himself as to the bear. "But that doesn't matter."

The bear looked up at him again, its tired eyes blinking slowly. "Maybe it doesn't."

The bear let out a long, sorrowful sigh, its eyes distant. "Everything's bad," it muttered, its voice thick with despair. "My life, my appearance... the other bears avoid me. I've lost the will to even try anymore. I'm just... broken. There's nothing good left."

Viraj shook his head slowly, his gaze steady. "You don't see it, do you?" he said softly. "You've been hurt, yes. You've been through things that most can't imagine. But that doesn't mean everything is bad. You've survived. That's something. Not everyone can say that."

The bear's gaze flickered. "Survived? That's all? Just surviving? I don't want to live like this. I don't want to be this... this shadow of what I could have been. Why even bother?"

Viraj stepped closer, his voice calm but firm. "Because there's more to life than what you've been through. Because being alive means you have the chance to change. To grow. To see the world beyond the pain. You may not be able to erase what's happened, but you can still shape your future. It's not about being perfect, it's about finding peace in who you are."

The bear seemed to ponder this, its tired eyes softening just slightly. "But no one cares. No one wants me. Not the other bears, not even the humans. I'm not wanted. I'm just a scarred, ugly thing."

Viraj knelt down to the bear's level, speaking quietly but with a gentle intensity. "Do you really think no one cares? Look at me. I've been called ugly, rejected, laughed at, just like you. But I found my place, in my own way. I found peace here, in the quiet of nature, where it doesn't matter how I look, just what I say. I found purpose. You can too, if you let yourself."

The bear shifted, its heavy body stiffening as it took in Viraj's words. It looked down at its own battered form, its eyes tracing the scars that marred its once-mighty frame. "I don't know," it murmured. "I don't know if I can. Everything just feels too hard. Too much pain, too many scars."

Viraj reached out a hand, a silent gesture of understanding. "It's okay to feel that way. It's okay to be broken. But don't let that define you. You're still here. You're still breathing. You can still find the beauty in the small things, the things that the world misses. The sound of the river, the rustling of the leaves. Sometimes, that's enough."

The bear let out a deep breath, but instead of responding with gratitude, it gave a low, gruff laugh, shaking its head. "You speak like it's all so simple. Like I can just wake up one day and forget everything I've been through. Like the world's suddenly going to be kind. But I know better." It sighed heavily, eyes dull with resignation. "This is just who I am now. No one can change that. Not you, not anyone."

Viraj fell silent, his hand still hovering in the air, unsure how to reach the bear any further. The truth of what the bear had said hung in the air like a cloud, heavy and undeniable. The poet's words, as hopeful as they were, couldn't erase the pain the bear had lived through.

Finally, the bear turned its massive head, casting one last glance at Viraj. "You keep your peace, poet. It's a nice dream... but it's not for me." Without another word, it began to lumber toward the edge of the village, its steps heavy, the scars on its body dragging with each movement.

Viraj watched silently, the quiet between them stretching out. As the bear disappeared into the shadows of the forest, he was left standing alone, the weight of their conversation hanging in the air, unanswered. The world was cruel, yes—but perhaps, for some, that cruelty would always be too much to overcome.

Viraj turned away, the distant murmur of the river the only sound to fill the quiet space left by the bear's departure.

A few days later, Viraj sat alone on a bench, facing the beach. He had come to the city to buy a new diary and a bundle of pens, like he always did when they ran out. His current diary was filled, the last pages scrawled with his thoughts, his poems, and the quiet moments he had experienced in Khadipur. The pens he had used were now dry, their ink long gone. The city, with all its noise and chaos, was always his destination for these small essentials, even though he hated every moment of it. It was a necessary part of his cycle—come to the city, gather what he needed, and then return to the peace of the village.

As Viraj sat there, the crowd around him continued on, laughing and making fun of him. He didn't care anymore. No one ever sat next to him. They all passed by, eyes averted, some snickering under their breath. It wasn't new. His quietness, his appearance, always made him an outsider. He watched the waves crash against the shore, seeking solace in their rhythm, but the laughter and mockery from the crowd lingered.

The beach was as busy as ever. People walked by in groups, laughing, chatting, unaware of the quiet man sitting on the bench. They never sat beside him. No one ever did. Viraj was used to it by now, the way people avoided him, the way they mocked his appearance, his quietness, his oddness. He glanced at the waves crashing against the shore, the rhythm soothing for a moment before the noise of the city flooded back into his mind.

As he sat there, lost in his thoughts, a man approached and unexpectedly sat down beside him on the bench. Viraj turned, surprised. The man was older, dressed in a simple jacket, and he didn't seem to mind the people bustling around him. What struck Viraj immediately, though, was that the man's eyes were blank, unseeing. The man was blind.

Viraj opened his mouth to say something, but the blind man spoke first, his voice warm and calm. "Hello."

Viraj blinked, still unsure how to respond. "You... can't see me, can you?" he asked cautiously.

The blind man smiled, his head tilting slightly. "I don't need to see you to know you're there," he said simply. "I can feel your presence. It's enough."

Viraj stared at the man, trying to make sense of what he'd just said. "You can feel... me?" he asked, puzzled.

"Yes," the man replied, his tone light and unbothered. "We all have a way of sensing the world, even without our eyes. It's not about sight, it's about connection."

Viraj was taken aback. He had never thought of it that way. He had always believed his own isolation was a matter of being unseen, of blending into the background. But the blind man—this stranger—had seen something in him, something that no one else had.

For a few moments, the two sat in silence, just listening to the waves, the distant chatter of people walking by, and the occasional seagull's cry. Viraj glanced at the blind man, noting how relaxed he seemed despite the chaos around them.

Finally, the blind man spoke again. "Tell me, how does the world look to you?"

Viraj hesitated, unsure of how to answer. "Well..." he began slowly, "there's the beach, with the waves crashing against the shore. The sun reflects off the water, making it shimmer. The sky is mostly blue, but there are clouds drifting by. Some people walk by, laughing, others seem too serious. The buildings are tall, and the noise... the noise never stops. It's all too much, too loud. But in the middle of all that, there's something calming. Like a rhythm to it, if you listen closely."

The blind man nodded, his lips curving into a small smile. "It sounds beautiful," he said, his voice filled with genuine admiration. "I envy the way you see the world."

Viraj chuckled bitterly, his gaze drifting back to the horizon. "It's not as beautiful as it sounds. There's too much noise, too much chaos. People only see what's in front of them, and no one ever notices me. I'm just... there. A part of the background."

The blind man tilted his head again, sensing the shift in Viraj's tone. "What do you mean? You feel like you're invisible?"

Viraj nodded, his voice tinged with frustration. "Yes, exactly. I've spent my whole life trying to fit in, trying to be part of something, but no one ever accepts me. In the city, I'm just part of the crowd. I'm not even real to them. I move through the noise, unnoticed, invisible. In the village, it's no better. They mock me for being different, for writing poetry, for being so quiet. I don't fit anywhere. I'm not good enough for either place."

The blind man's face softened, and for a moment, Viraj could feel an understanding radiating from him, a depth of feeling that went beyond words. "You feel like you don't belong, like you're stuck between two worlds," the blind man said gently.

"Exactly," Viraj replied, his voice breaking slightly. "It's like I'm caught between two places that aren't really mine. And I'm always alone. Always."

The blind man remained silent for a while, as if weighing Viraj's words. Then, with a thoughtful expression, he said, "But you could change that. You could let go of that anger, you know. The way you're holding onto it isn't doing you any good."

Viraj looked at him sharply. "You think I don't know that? You think I don't understand the anger I carry? It's not like I chose it. It's just there, inside me. I can't escape it."

The blind man's face softened further, his tone calm yet firm. "You think holding onto it is the answer? Anger's a poison, my friend. It doesn't change anything. It doesn't help anyone, especially not you."

Viraj's jaw tightened, his voice growing more intense. "You don't understand. You don't know what it's like, to be laughed at, to be humiliated, to be mocked for something you can't change. How do you deal with that? How do you keep going when people treat you like you don't exist? I'm angry because I'm tired. I'm tired of being ignored, of being overlooked, of being nothing but a shadow in a world full of bright lights."

The blind man's expression remained calm, almost serene. "I do understand," he said quietly. "Not in the way you think, but I understand. I've known pain. I've known what it feels like to be looked at like I'm invisible. But I've also learned that letting that pain control me doesn't make it better. It just makes it worse."

Viraj scoffed, shaking his head. "And what should I do? Let it go? Pretend everything's fine when it's not? Pretend I'm not hurt when I am?"

The blind man didn't flinch. "Not let it go, but change how you carry it. You don't have to forget the pain, but you can choose how you respond to it. You can choose to use it, to let it teach you something, instead of letting it eat you up inside."

Viraj turned away, looking at the people walking by, none of them paying any attention to him, none of them even noticing the conversation he was having with a stranger. His frustration grew, his voice thick with emotion. "How do you do that? How do you stop letting the world's cruelty change who you are? How do you stop the pain from making you... like them? How do you not become bitter?"

The blind man smiled softly. "You stop when you realize that the world's cruelty isn't a reflection of who you are. It's a reflection of them. People are cruel because they're hurting. You're not responsible for their pain, only how you choose to react to it."

Viraj was silent for a long moment, considering the words. "So, you're saying I should just let it all go? Forget the insults, forget the laughter, forget the loneliness?"

The blind man leaned in slightly, his voice soft but insistent. "No. I'm not saying forget. I'm saying that you need to stop letting it control you. You need to take it and turn it into something that helps you grow. You don't have to let it shape you into bitterness. You can be better than that."

Viraj shook his head slowly, feeling an internal tug. "It's not that simple. It's hard. It's so hard to let go of all the years of pain. It's hard to stop hating the world for how it's treated me."

The blind man chuckled lightly, his voice still filled with warmth. "I never said it was easy. But it's worth it. You have a choice in how you move forward. You can either stay trapped in the anger, or you can choose to let the pain make you stronger, not weaker."

Viraj paused, feeling a strange weight lift off his chest, though just slightly. There was a quietness inside him, an openness to the idea that maybe, just maybe, there was another way to live, a way he hadn't seen before.

The blind man rose to his feet, and Viraj stood with him, still processing the conversation. "Before I go," the blind man said with a grin, "one more thing. Eat vegetables. They're good for you."

Viraj blinked, momentarily thrown off by the strange advice. "Vegetables? What does that even mean?"

The blind man laughed heartily. "It means that sometimes, the simplest things are the most important. Life isn't always what you expect, but if you learn to appreciate it, you'll find the sweetness in it."

Viraj frowned, not quite getting the point. "You're saying I should just accept everything, like it's all okay?"

The blind man's eyes twinkled, and he tapped his cane against the ground. "I'm saying that sometimes, you have to look at the bigger picture. You can't always change what's around you, but you can change how you see it."

Viraj shook his head, not entirely convinced, but there was a flicker of something in him, a shift. The blind man's words had planted a seed, and though it felt strange, it felt like the start of something.

The blind man smiled one last time, gave a final wave, and walked off, tapping his cane gently as he disappeared into the crowd. Viraj stood still, feeling a strange mixture of calm and uncertainty, but somewhere deep inside, he knew the man had been right. There was more to life than the pain he had carried for so long. He didn't know exactly how to make it work, but maybe—just maybe—he could start looking for the good, even in the smallest moments.

The bus back to the village was crowded as usual, the air thick with the smell of sweat and dust. Viraj sat by the window, his face pressed against the cool glass, staring out at the blur of buildings and streets as they passed by. The world outside seemed far away, a world that moved quickly and without care, while inside, he felt the weight of the day's conversation lingering in his mind.

The blind man's words echoed in his thoughts. *You have a choice in how you move forward.* Viraj shifted in his seat, feeling the familiar ache of loneliness rise in his chest. The noise of the bus, the chatter of the other passengers, all seemed distant. He was alone, but not in the usual way. It was a kind of solitude that felt deeper, more introspective.

The conversation with the old man had unsettled him, in a way he hadn't expected. For years, Viraj had lived with anger and hurt, letting them define him. The world had never been kind to him, and he had built walls around himself to protect against the constant sting of rejection. *People are cruel because they're hurting,* the blind man had said. *You're not responsible for their pain, only how you choose to react to it.*

Viraj frowned. He had always blamed the world for what had happened to him. The mockery in the village. The isolation in the city. The cruelty that seemed to follow him wherever he went. How could he not be angry? How could he not feel betrayed by everything and everyone?

And yet, there was something in the blind man's words that made him question it all. Could he really change how he saw things? Could he choose to not let the world's cruelty define him? Could he—after all these years—start seeing the good in the world, despite the pain?

He shifted again, glancing out the window at the familiar fields and trees that lined the road back to his village. His mind wandered to the people there, the same faces he had seen for years, the same people who mocked him, who never understood him. Would they ever change? Would he ever change?

As the bus rumbled on, Viraj closed his eyes for a moment, his hand gripping the edge of the seat. The old man had been right about one thing: life wasn't easy. The pain wasn't something you could simply let go of, not all at once. It would take time, and maybe more than time, it would take a willingness to face the hurt, to look it in the eye and say, *I won't let you control me anymore.*

He sighed, staring out at the blur of the world passing by. The poet had always been a quiet observer, someone who felt the weight of every word, every glance, every unspoken judgment. It wasn't that he wanted to be angry, but anger had been his shield, his defense against a world that had never been kind to him.

But maybe, just maybe, there was a way to live without that shield. Maybe he didn't have to be defined by the way people saw him or the way they treated him. Maybe, just maybe, there was more to life than the bitterness he had carried for so long.

The bus jolted as it hit a bump in the road, pulling Viraj from his thoughts. He sat up straighter, feeling the familiar weight of the notebook tucked into his bag. It was still there, his constant companion. But now, for the first time in a long while, it didn't feel as heavy. Maybe it was time to write something different, something that reflected not just the pain, but the possibility of something better.

As the bus neared the village, Viraj felt the smallest flicker of hope deep inside him, a hope he had long since buried. The road ahead was still uncertain, but for the first time, he was willing to take a step forward, even if it was just one small step. And as the bus slowed to a stop, he took a deep breath, ready to face whatever came next.

Meanwhile, the bear lumbered through the dense forest, his mind clouded with frustration. The sunlight barely filtered through the towering trees as he approached the small den he shared with his mother. She was sitting inside, her fur dull and streaked with age, gnawing idly on the remains of a fish. When she saw him enter, her sharp eyes narrowed.

"Where have you been?" she asked, her tone sharp with worry. "I've told you not to wander off like that. The forest is dangerous enough without you going missing."

The bear hesitated, unsure of how to begin. But he wasn't a cub anymore, and the day's events were too significant to keep to himself. He sat down heavily, his old wounds stinging slightly from the journey.

"I went to the village," he said finally, his voice low.

His mother froze, her jaws ceasing their work on the fish. "The *village*?" she repeated, her voice rising. "What were you thinking? That's no place for a bear! Have you lost your mind?"

"I talked to someone there," he said, his tone defensive. "A man. A poet. He wasn't like the others. He didn't scream or run. He just... listened."

The old bear's expression shifted from shock to a mixture of concern and anger. "You *talked* to a human? You think that's something to be proud of? They're the reason you're like this! Those wounds, your scars—do you think they care? They see us as monsters, and you're giving them a reason to get even closer to you!"

The younger bear's claws scraped against the dirt floor as he lashed out. "It's not like the animals here treat me any better! Do you think I don't notice the way they look at me? The whispers, the snickers? I'm a joke to them! I've been mocked and pushed away my whole life. At least the poet didn't make me feel... like a freak."

His mother's eyes softened for a moment, but her voice remained firm. "I know it's hard, but the forest is our home. You don't belong in their world, and they don't belong in ours. That poet might seem kind, but humans are unpredictable. They destroy everything they touch. I won't let you put yourself in danger again."

"Danger?" the bear snapped. "I live in danger every day, Ma. Not just from humans, but from the other animals, from myself. You think staying here protects me? It doesn't. I'm suffocating in this place, in this life."

His mother's voice broke as she tried to reason with him. "You're all I have left. You think it's easy for me to see you like this? To watch you suffer and not be able to help? I've tried to protect you from the world, to keep you safe—"

"Safe from what?" the bear interrupted, rising to his feet. "From the humans, from the forest, from the truth? I don't want your protection, Ma. I want to live. To feel like I matter. And if that means going back to the village, then so be it."

"You will *not* go back there," his mother growled, her tone final. "I forbid it."

The bear's heart pounded with frustration, his breath coming in sharp bursts. "You can't control me forever," he said, his voice shaking. "I'm not a cub anymore. I don't care if you or anyone else thinks I'm wrong. I'm going."

Before his mother could respond, he turned and bolted out of the den, his massive paws thudding against the earth. His mother's voice called after him, desperate and filled with anguish, but he didn't stop.

The cool air of the forest whipped past him as he charged toward the village, anger and defiance driving every step. He didn't know what he expected to find there—acceptance, understanding, maybe even the poet—but he knew he couldn't stay in the forest any longer. Not when it felt like the walls were closing in on him.

And so, as the shadows of the trees thinned and the faint outlines of the village appeared in the distance, the bear pushed forward, determined to find something—anything—that would make his life feel a little less lonely.

The bear trudged through the forest, his frustration simmering beneath his heavy steps. The echoes of his argument with his mother still lingered in his mind, a storm of emotions he couldn't quiet. As he reached the river, the cool morning air hit him, and for a moment, he just stood there, the vast expanse of water stretching before him.

Then, across the river, he spotted a familiar figure.

The poet.

But something was different. The poet wasn't wandering with his notebook or muttering lines of verse. He was walking purposefully, his back straight, a suitcase in one hand and a bulging bag slung over his shoulder. The bear tilted his head, confused. The poet was heading in the opposite direction, away from the village.

The bear's heart sank as he realized what this meant. The poet was leaving.

From his place by the riverbank, the bear watched as the poet reached the top of a hill. There, the man paused and turned to glance back at the village one last time. It was a small gesture, but the bear felt its weight. Without hesitation, the poet turned and disappeared over the ridge, his silhouette swallowed by the rising sun.

The bear stared at the empty spot where the poet had been, his chest tightening. He had come all this way, hoping to find someone who understood his pain, only to see that person walking away from everything the bear thought tethered them together.

Hours earlier, on a rattling bus winding through narrow roads, Viraj sat by a window, gazing out at the passing countryside. His suitcase rested at his feet, the bag of notebooks and pens beside it.

He had always dreaded leaving the village, but this time was different. He wasn't going to the city for supplies and planning a quiet return. He was leaving for good.

The decision had come slowly, like the soft erosion of a dam holding back his dreams. Year after year, he had stayed in the village, enduring the ridicule and isolation because he thought it was where he had to be—a retreat from a cruel city that had scarred him in his youth. But staying had become its own kind of prison.

The blind man's words echoed in his mind. *You can let the world define you, or you can define yourself.*

The city was where his heart truly belonged. It wasn't perfect—nothing ever was—but it was where stories began. The faces, the noise, the ever-changing tide of life, raw and unfiltered—it was where he could find inspiration and maybe even a sense of belonging.

For too long, he had let the cruelty of others dictate his life. Not anymore.

Viraj leaned back against the worn seat, clutching his bag of fresh notebooks. This time, he was going to the city not to escape but to embrace it.

The bear stood at the riverbank, his heart sinking as he watched the poet disappear over the hill. For a moment, he felt the weight of loneliness press down on him, heavy and suffocating. He had run all this way, hoping to find the only creature who had ever truly listened to him, only to discover that the poet was leaving too.

The poet was heading to a place he longed for, a place where he believed he belonged. And the bear? He was here, on the edge of the forest, torn between the world that had hurt him and the world that had never truly welcomed him.

The bear looked down at his reflection in the river—scarred, bruised, and battered, but still standing. He let out a long, heavy breath, the cool air stinging his lungs. Slowly, he turned away from the village and the river.

He didn't look back as he lumbered into the forest, his massive paws sinking into the soft earth.

Somewhere in the distance, the poet walked toward the city, his suitcase swinging with each step, his heart lighter than it had been in years.

Two souls, walking in opposite directions, both searching for the place where they belonged.

The river flowed on, quiet and eternal, carrying with it the unspoken stories of those who came and went.

The End.

CHAPTER II

The Poet & His Poems

ONE DAY-
   I'll never stop waiting
For that day to arrive,
One with the solutions,
Solutions to survive
   Survive this mess
Which someone else threw at my plate,
The only sin I ever did
Was being too late,
   Is late the right word?
Or should I say never?
Because I still haven't told her,
And it will be that way forever,
   Because it only takes one day
To change someone's life,
A simple gesture, a word of hope
Can cut through the strife,
   I may have made mistakes,
I may have been cursed,
I may have faced the darkness,
I may have felt the worst,
   I may rise from the ashes,
I may find my own way,
I may not like the journey,
I may bleed further each day,
   But I still wait
For that one day to arrive,
Kill all my mistakes

Darted at the board,
    Left for me to trace,
Forced into my throat,
I keep screaming the name of God,
As if I have no other choice,
    Searching for answers in the silence,
Yearning for a guiding voice
    All these pages will be wasted
And so will I,
The sweet smell of success that I never tasted
And won't taste until I die,
    But I still wait for the day
To come and behold,
Was it a mistake I didn't join the fray?
Find a courage untold,
    As I lay on the grass
I look at the moon,
I watch my mistakes pass,
Mistakes I made too soon,
    The day I wait for
May never arrive,
So, I'll live through this night,
Wait for the sun to rise
    But it won't rise anymore
Be it the sun or my tears,
So, I'll sit idle through this night
Knowing I never conquered my fears
    Fears embedded into my mind,
A mind beyond my hands,
My gleamy eyes still shined,
For a weak mind tied with strands,
    Maybe cut all my ties?
Maybe tie some more?

Maybe tie some better?
Maybe tie some with you?
    I know I was too late,
I know I'm a stranger,
Lost in the echoes of time,
Navigating through danger,
    I see myself tied to a chair
With an axe on my neck,
I see the sun rise elsewhere
As hope flickers in the wreck,
    I wanted to check if this is the day,
The day I waited for,
I see the axe being raised by the stray,
And my neck he is aiming for,
    I never saw that day arrive
To end all my problems,
Only endless nights of doubt
And hopes that feel like phantoms,
    But now I need not worry
Because I now rest endless,
The line between life and death is now blurry
I'm weak because I lie pen-less,
    The pen was always mightier
Because I never held a sword,
Crafting tales of battles fought,
Where words became my shield and ward,
    Was Shakespeare correct?
Will this poem last forever?
Will there be an ending to these pages?
End it now or write forever?
    But I always cared what others said,
I never cared about my ideas,
Angrily swinging the belt upon the belt,

Because I have now ran out of ideas,
    Blood and tears everywhere
But I sat there still,
Blood and tears everywhere
Of emotions I had to kill,
    Killed to hide from the world
And from you,
I still think deep inside,
Think about the few,
    The few moments which I spent with you,
I spoiled my innocent heart
I spoiled my tender skin
To fall in love with you,
    Even God admires his creations
But doesn't admire me,
God is admired by generations
Who don't admire me,
    Is that it? I ask,
As I see the sun rise and kill the rain,
Is this the day I waited for?
Or will I have to wait again?
    But as the dawn creeps in, I feel the chill,
A reminder that hope can be cruel and stark,
The dreams I once clung to fade, faint and still,
As I sit in the shadows, waiting for light in the dark.

. . .

EVEN IF-
    Even if a comet to end the world was travelling the skies
And it looked as beautiful as the bracelet you wear,
I'd choose to look at the comet through the reflection of
your eyes

And we'll be turned to ashes right then and there,
    This situationship I'm trapped in confuses me
The dancing sparkle in your eyes which amuses me,
Caught in a web of what might never be
Is this love or just a breeze, is what confuses me,
    I can easily fill the wound you left in my heart
But I won't because it's the last memory of yours before we
fell apart,
Others hugged you while I was hesitant to touch
Afraid that a single embrace would mean too much,
    Now you sit as your coffee is colding
And various packets of cigarettes I lit,
I feel the book of our story finally folding
Now with a sigh in wait for its sequel I sit.

● ● ●

SOMETIMES-
    Sometimes I find myself begging for love,
Sometimes I can't even bother.
Sometimes I plead to the one up above
To give all my sins a slaughter.
    Sometimes I wish to be held high,
Otherwise, I wish to be alone.
Sometimes I want to fly and touch the sky,
Otherwise, peace holds me on the ground I roam.
    Sometimes I feel that the pen is my greatest friend,
Otherwise, I look at it as a rival.
Pen's a friend which taught me friendship must end —
The pen is the lone cause of my survival.
    I helped others find their paths,
Now among those same trails I'm entangled.
To survive the river of sadness, I built rafts —
Rafts of emotions I killed and strangled.

And now I put my pen down,
Knowing it separated me from the herd.

• • •

WAKE UP-
I woke up
To the sound of a scream.
I closed my eyes,
Prayed for it all to be a dream.
But I knew it was real —
I could feel it.
They eat my feelings as a meal,
And my happiness? They steal it.
Which has now made me empty,
And confused as well.
Now I have no other friend
For my story to tell.
So I kept it in my mind,
Hoping I'll find someone one day.
But nobody did I find,
To tell my story someday.
And I just kept waiting —
And I still am.
I feel my happiness fading,
But I smile, because I still can.
God has helped me various times before,
But why not now, when I need Him most?
God has answered various times before —
Now I'm lost, like a wandering ghost.
The second I think I'm being helped,
Next thing I see is that I'm falling.
I cursed the world and thought it would melt,
And now, back to the world, I'm crawling.

Do you really want me to wake up again?
Or is it just a lie to ease my pain?
I'm broken — will you build me up again?
And sit beside me as the clouds rain?
I will fix all my issues.
I will find the solutions.
With courage as my compass,
And hope to guide my resolutions.
I will make my parents happy.
I will make my sister proud.
I will walk the streets with success —
But you'll stare at me with a glimpse of doubt.
This poem will end,
And so will my time.
Everyone will lose a friend,
And soon will end this rhyme.
Because I'm no hero.
I'm not even a proper human.
Lost in the shadows of fright,
Looking for my own fusion.
But I can't wake up —
Because in my dreams, I have you.
Where every moment feels real,
And my fears fade from view.
Will I wake up again?
Or live in my dream?
Watch the clouds rain,
My arms clenched, with you in between.

• • •

Broken Mirrors–
I look into broken mirrors,
Shattered shards of former fears,

Reflections cracked, a fractured face,
Lost somewhere without a trace,
   Each piece shows a different me,
Fragments of what I used to be,
Some hold hope, some hold despair,
Some whisper truths I cannot bear,
   I try to glue them back again,
But broken mirrors always stain,
No matter how I try to mend,
The cracks remind me of the end,
   Yet in this broken glass I see,
A thousand versions of the "me,"
And maybe in this shattered art,
Lies the courage to restart.

• • •

Faded Lights-
   Faded lights in empty rooms,
Shadows creeping under closed doors,
Echoes of the laughter once we knew,
Whispering stories I wish I never heard before,
   I trace the cracks along the wall,
To words I never spoke or dared to hear,
Each one a scar, a silent call,
To days I lost and nights I feared,
   I watch the moon fade into dawn,
But in this fading light I find,
Knowing soon the night will be gone,
The broken pieces of my mind,
   The light once bright now barely glows,
While I'm still caught inside this haze,
In rooms where no one ever knows,
Counting down the empty days,

Maybe hope is just a ghost,
A spark that flickered, then withdrew,
A fading dream I loved the most,
Leaving silence where life once grew,
I reach for shadows on the floor,
Fingers brushing empty air,
Grasping at what is no more,
Touching nothing but despair,
I wonder if the light will shine,
Or will it dim and slowly die,
Again upon this heart of mine,
A forgotten spark beneath the sky,
But still, I wait for dawn to break,
The wounds that never let me sleep,
For something more than this to take,
The pain that lingers, soft and deep,
And though the night seems never-ending,
A whisper that might conquer all,
And broken lights refuse to mending,
I hold a flicker, faint and small,
For faded lights may yet ignite,
I hope for one more brightened day,
A blaze that scatters endless night,
And though I've stumbled, lost my way.

• • •

The Waiting Room-
So here I stay, I wait, I dream,
With hands that tremble at the light,
Though nothing's ever as it seems,
I beg the stars to end the night.
A fragile thread, a whispered plea,
Is all I clutch beneath my chest,

That someday soon, I will be free—
But freedom may just mean I rest.
　　I watched them call another name,
And not my own—it never was,
Like fading credits from a frame,
Where I was ghosted from the cause.
　　My number stayed upon the board,
But no one came to call it out,
The nurse moved on without a word,
My hope replaced by silent doubt.
　　The room grew cold, the lights went dim,
The others left, but I remained,
Still speaking words that felt like hymn,
To ears that time itself had drained.
　　I thought I'd rise, I thought I'd go,
But something pulled me deeper down,
As if the waiting was the show—
And I, the fool who wore the crown.
　　A final tear, a silent fall,
My breath grew still, my thoughts went wide,
I saw the door, I saw the hall—
And then the light left from my side.
　　They found me slumped beside the chair,
A note clenched tight in frozen hand,
"I waited long, but none were there—
So now I leave. Please understand."
　　And somewhere in that silent room,
The clock kept ticking, unaware,
While outside bloomed the springtime bloom,
Inside, I vanished with the air.

• • •

The Last Train Home-

The last train left at half past three,
I watched it vanish down the track,
The station lights blinked silently,
But none could bring the silence back.

My coat was damp, my hands were bare,
The rain slipped down my shadow's face,
I stood alone, stripped of all care,
As time dissolved without a trace.

The benches creaked with ghostly sound,
As if the night could feel regret,
Of all the souls that passed this ground,
And all the ones it won't forget.

I held a letter in my hand,
Unsent, unopened, out of fear,
A shaky note I couldn't stand—
Addressed to you, but never near.

I wrote it when I missed your voice,
And missed the way you'd tilt your head,
Before you made your final choice,
To leave my thoughts and love for dead.

"I'm sorry" was the first I wrote,
"I never meant to be too late,"
But sorrow caught inside my throat,
And sealed the letter up with fate.

I meant to board and say it all—
I truly did, I swear I tried,
But courage dies when shadows fall,
And hearts break slow, and dreams have lied.

A family boarded holding hands,
A child asleep on someone's arm,
And I just watched from where I stand,
A ghost outside their circle's warm.

The intercom, a lifeless hum,
Announced a train I wouldn't take,
I had the time, but stayed numb,
And let another good thing break.

The guard approached—he looked away,
As if my grief could be contagious,
He'd seen this scene on one more day,
The broken ones, the almost-courageous.

The clock hands bled into the past,
The present lost its pulse and sound,
The empty tracks, too still, too vast—
And I remained, not homeward bound.

I thought of all the things you said,
The half-smiles, and the shared cold tea,
And how the world just moved ahead,
But froze in place for only me.

You said, "There's beauty in the break,"
But all I found were jagged lines,
And every laugh we didn't fake,
Still echoes through these empty signs.

I dreamed that you might run to me,
With wind behind your soaked-up coat,
And whisper, "Love, just let it be,"
And place your hand around my throat—

Not in anger, but to check,
If life still lived within this shell,
If there was time left to protect,
Or if I'd sunk too deep in hell.

But you don't come. You never do.
The platform fades beneath my shoes.
I close my eyes and think of you,
And every way I had to lose.

An old man offers me his seat,
I smile and shake my heavy head,
He doesn't know I've faced defeat—
Or maybe that's the thing he read.

He says, "The trains will come again,"
And then he nods, and walks away,
But I don't trust the clocks or men,
Or words that try to make me stay.

The wind picks up, the letter tears—
It flies and lands along the track,
I chase it down through vacant stares,
But never get the paper back.

I watch it vanish down the line,
Like you, like hope, like every chance,
Like all the stars I called "still mine"
Now hidden in a different dance.

The sun begins to rise, somehow,
Though no one asked it to appear,
And I'm still standing, lost in vow,
Still choking on what brought me here.

And in that light—so soft, so cruel—
I see a version of myself,
A child, naïve, a broken fool,
Still putting dreams back on the shelf.

I walk the edge, I scan the stone,
And find my name scratched faint and grey,
Perhaps I've been here all alone,
Perhaps I died some yesterday.

The screen still lists departures due,
But never lists a place called peace,
I wish I knew if you once knew,
That loving me meant no release.

The train returns, all empty seats,
A final call, a quiet tone,
And as it halts, the silence greets
The boy who's always been alone.
   I step aboard—no bags, no fight—
Just one more breath beneath my mask,
And hope the shadows treat me right,
And don't return to ask or task.
   I take a seat, the doors slide in,
No one sits near, no eyes to meet,
And as the engine starts to spin,
I feel my heartbeat lose its beat.
   The train pulls out into the dusk,
And through the glass I see the rain,
I rest my head against the husk
Of all the poems born from pain.
   A final thought, one last refrain—
If I had loved myself back then,
Would I still board this endless train,
Or wait for you to try again?

• • •

The Home I Knew-
   I walked down the street where I once felt known,
Now each step sounds like a dial tone.
The lamps still flicker in polite routine,
But their light doesn't reach where I've been.
   The windows reflect a version of me,
But I'm a stranger in every memory.
The paint on the walls peels like old skin,
And silence is louder than it's ever been.
   There's a book on the shelf I never wrote,
Its pages blank, but it still takes note.

Of every dream I abandoned mid-page,
Of every war I fought inside a cage.
	They called this place a haven,
But I only found doors that wouldn't open.
Every hallway leads to a mirror,
And every mirror just makes it clearer.
	I didn't come here to be found —
I came to bury the version of me that drowned.
The one who smiled too often out of fear,
Who waited for a voice he'd never hear.
	Time moves here like a stubborn clock,
Each tick another part I unlock.
But nothing's left behind the door,
Just echoes dancing across the floor.
	I once thought pain made you stronger,
That the broken survive just a little longer.
But all it did was make me quiet —
A whisper lost in a world of riot.
	The city outside doesn't know my name,
I pass through it like static in the rain.
They say everyone's chasing something true,
But I lost the chase the day I lost you.
	Not a person, not a face —
Just the feeling of being in the right place.
A chair that fits, a sky that stays,
A voice that doesn't look away.
	There's a fire I can't feel anymore,
I sit beside it, numb to the core.
It burns like the years I let go,
Like letters returned from long ago.
	The lights are on — I keep them that way,
Hoping someone will stop and say
"Are you okay?" — but no one does.

They never ask. They never was.
    I left notes for the world in invisible ink,
Hid my truth where no one would think.
I screamed in poems and bled in prose,
But no one reads what no one knows.
    I built a room inside my head,
Where I talk to the versions of me that are dead.
We sit in silence, sometimes in song,
All wondering how we got it so wrong.
    And if I go missing —
No searchlight, no listing.
Just a headline in some quiet domain:
"Another boy lost in his own name."
    But I'm not lost. I'm just not found.
I'm the scream that made no sound.
I'm the house that looked like home,
With lights still on —
But no one's ever home.

• • •

Thank You!

Thank You for Reading

Thank you so much for taking the time to read my book. Your support means the world to me! This project was a labor of love, and I hope it brought you some joy, thought, or inspiration along the way.

Right now, I'm working on something bigger and even better—a new fiction project that I'm really excited about. I can't wait to share that story with you soon.

Until then, take care and keep reading. Goodbye for now.

Hail Ironvale!

www.ingramcontent.com/pod-product-compliance
Lightning Source LLC
Chambersburg PA
CBHW020515160726
47991CB00007B/2959